I knew the books would be good, but I didn't realize how good.

— Night Stalkers series, Kirkus Reviews

Buchman mixes adrenalin-spiking battles and brusque military jargon with a sensitive approach.

— Publishers Weekly

13 times "Top Pick of the Month"

— Night Owl Reviews

PRAISE FOR M. L. BUCHMAN

Tom Clancy fans open to a strong female lead will clamor for more.

— *Drone*, Publishers Weekly

Superb!

— *Drone*, Booklist starred review

The best military thriller I've read in a very long time. Love the female characters.

— *Drone*, Sheldon McArthur, founder of The Mystery Bookstore, LA

A fabulous soaring thriller.

— *Take Over at Midnight*, Midwest Book Review

Meticulously researched, hard-hitting, and suspenseful.

— *Pure Heat*, Publishers Weekly, starred review

Expert technical details abound, as do realistic military missions with superb imagery that will have readers feeling as if they are right there in the midst and on the edges of their seats.

— *Light Up the Night,* RT Reviews, 4 1/2 stars

Buchman has catapulted his way to the top tier of my favorite authors.

— Fresh Fiction

Nonstop action that will keep readers on the edge of their seats.

— *Take Over at Midnight,* Library Journal

M L. Buchman's ability to keep the reader right in the middle of the action is amazing.

— Long and Short Reviews

The only thing you'll ask yourself is, "When does the next one come out?"

— *Wait Until Midnight,* RT Reviews, 4 stars

The first...of (a) stellar, long-running (military) romantic suspense series.

— *The Night is Mine,* Booklist, "The 20 Best Romantic Suspense Novels: Modern Masterpieces"

SURVIVE UNTIL THE FINAL SCENE

A NIGHT STALKERS CSAR STORY

M. L. BUCHMAN

Published by Buchman Bookworks, Inc.

Receive a free book and discover more by this author at: www.mlbuchman.com

Cover images:

Desert Hiking Trail with Red Cliffs © kvddesign | DepositPhotos

Evening Desert © Kokhanchikov | DepositPhotos

US Army UH-60 Black Hawk helicopter © Michael Kaplan | Wikimedia

SIGN UP FOR M. L. BUCHMAN'S NEWSLETTER TODAY

and receive:

Release News

Free Short Stories

a Free Book

Get your free book today. Do it now.

free-book.mlbuchman.com

Other works by M. L. Buchman: *(* - also in audio)*

Action-Adventure Thrillers

Dead Chef

One Chef!
Two Chef!

Miranda Chase

*Drone**
*Thunderbolt**
*Condor**
*Ghostrider**

Romantic Suspense

Delta Force

*Target Engaged**
*Heart Strike**
*Wild Justice**
*Midnight Trust**

Firehawks

MAIN FLIGHT

Pure Heat
Full Blaze
*Hot Point**
*Flash of Fire**
Wild Fire

SMOKEJUMPERS

*Wildfire at Dawn**
*Wildfire at Larch Creek**
*Wildfire on the Skagit**

The Night Stalkers

MAIN FLIGHT

The Night Is Mine
I Own the Dawn
Wait Until Dark
Take Over at Midnight
Light Up the Night
Bring On the Dusk
By Break of Day

AND THE NAVY

Christmas at Steel Beach
Christmas at Peleliu Cove

WHITE HOUSE HOLIDAY

*Daniel's Christmas**
*Frank's Independence Day**
*Peter's Christmas**
*Zachary's Christmas**
*Roy's Independence Day**
*Damien's Christmas**

5E

Target of the Heart
Target Lock on Love
Target of Mine
Target of One's Own

Shadow Force: Psi

*At the Slightest Sound**
*At the Quietest Word**
*At the Merest Glance**
*At the Clearest Sensation**

White House Protection Force

*Off the Leash**
*On Your Mark**
*In the Weeds**

Contemporary Romance

Eagle Cove

Return to Eagle Cove
Recipe for Eagle Cove
Longing for Eagle Cove
Keepsake for Eagle Cove

Henderson's Ranch

*Nathan's Big Sky**
*Big Sky, Loyal Heart**
*Big Sky Dog Whisperer**

Love Abroad

Heart of the Cotswolds: England
Path of Love: Cinque Terre, Italy

Other works by M. L. Buchman:

Contemporary Romance (cont)

Where Dreams

Where Dreams are Born
Where Dreams Reside
*Where Dreams Are of Christmas**
Where Dreams Unfold
Where Dreams Are Written

Science Fiction / Fantasy

Deities Anonymous

Cookbook from Hell: Reheated
Saviors 101

Single Titles

The Nara Reaction
Monk's Maze
the Me and Elsie Chronicles

Non-Fiction

Strategies for Success

Managing Your Inner Artist/Writer
*Estate Planning for Authors**
Character Voice
*Narrate and Record Your Own Audiobook**

Short Story Series by M. L. Buchman:

Romantic Suspense

Delta Force

Th Delta Force Shooters
The Delta Force Warriors

Firehawks

The Firehawks Lookouts
The Firehawks Hotshots
The Firebirds

The Night Stalkers

The Night Stalkers
The Night Stalkers 5E
The Night Stalkers CSAR
The Night Stalkers Wedding Stories

US Coast Guard

White House Protection Force

Contemporary Romance

Eagle Cove

Henderson's Ranch*

Where Dreams

Action-Adventure Thrillers

Dead Chef

Miranda Chase Origin

Science Fiction / Fantasy

Deities Anonymous

Other

The Future Night Stalkers
Single Titles

ABOUT THIS BOOK

The most dangerous mission of all: CSAR—Combat Search and Rescue.

Captain Kandace Eversmann's *plane goes down hard in the Somali desert. With her life expectancy falling by the minute, she uses tricks from her favorite movies in order to survive.*

Army Medic Bob Redford *has run out of reasons to stay in the Army. Until he must use his own love of movies to find the wounded pilot—fast. The race is on to beat an attacking militia that wants to take them both down before the final credits.*

1

Up until this very moment, Captain Kandace Eversmann had a soft spot for *Air America.* Even though she and the movie had been born in the same year, 1990, it was the first movie about airplanes she remembered.

Dad, a computer programmer, chose the Thursday night movies (a lot of espionage and thrillers) and Mom, a small-plane certified flight instructor, chose the Sunday night ones (a lot of flying). The best nights of her life were when the three of them curled up on the couch together with cookies or a slice of pie and watched a movie together.

Even now as a captain in the US Air Force, movie night served as her litmus test for boyfriends—a gauntlet very few survived.

Air America, a romp through the CIA's illegal flight operations in Laos during the Vietnam War, was the identifiable starting point of the journey that had made her an Air Force pilot.

And at this very moment, she *hated* that movie.

The opening had followed a big silver Fairchild C-123K Provider, twin-engine cargo plane across the sky. It zoomed low over the credits, barely above the treetops, making parachute deliveries of pigs, rice, and weapons.

Then, on its return to base, the Provider overflew a Laotian farmer strolling through his fields. He shouldered his prehistoric single-shot shotgun and fired once at the passing silver beast now high above. As he looked away and resumed his walk, the plane spilled out a smoke trail—ultimately crashing at the airport in a lethal ball of fire.

She remembered smiling, intrigued at the offhand power of the farmer.

One tiny shot, one giant plane. No way. It was too bizarre.

Kandace was presently pilot-in-command of the bigger, badder, four-engined descendant of the Provider, a C-130H Hercules.

A C-130 had dropped the life raft at the end of Bond's *You Only Live Twice,* and the MC-130 variant had rescued the President in *Air Force One.* It had been used in over two hundred movies and she'd seen most of them, even the bad ones. Kandace had always been drawn to the rescue and humanitarian role.

This moment had exactly the same feel as *Air America.*

But she sure wasn't smiling.

Her flight from the US Air Force base in Djibouti was carrying food and military supplies to the Kenyan troops of ANISOM. They were attempting to create some form of peace in Somalia. It had come down to either the fragile official government or the horror of the al-Shabaab religious fanatics. She knew where her vote lay, not that anyone was asking.

She'd been descending toward a landing in Saakow at the southern end of the country. No sneaking up from the sea because it was fifty miles inland. Instead, command had routed her directly overland from Djibouti, across a thousand miles of Ethiopian and Somalian nowhereness.

No hiding among other air traffic because there wasn't any. Saakow didn't have an airport. The only possible air approaches were for helicopters or short-field masters like the C-130.

This time she wasn't even scheduled to touch down. She'd do a combat drop at one meter above the desert, the cargo pallet yanked out of the rear of the plane by a parachute. The load would skid to a stop and she'd climb back up to altitude.

It was the high-end magic trick of the C-130, yet another reason she loved the plane so much.

But she hadn't been worried, everything was reported as being quiet in the area.

Not so much.

Out in the middle of that nowhereness, she must have overflown an al-Shabaab training camp. Or maybe just a bored, but very well-armed militia man.

Either way, her seventy-five-ton baby had just been shot by a technical—a pickup truck with a big machine gun mounted in the rear. Usually such jury-rigged military vehicles carried a .50 cal Browning machine gun. The chances of a few half-inch rounds seriously harming her baby were minimal. Especially as its effective range was barely a mile and she'd still been flying at two.

Somehow, this technical had mounted a massive Russian ZU-23 twin-barrel anti-aircraft autocannon on its bed. It tossed seven 23 mm rounds a second and could easily reach her altitude. At nearly an inch across and six long, they were far more damaging. Each delivered five times more energy to the target than the Browning as they'd smashed into her Number Two engine.

In her case? Too damaging.

If she leaned over far enough to look out her left-hand window, she could see the flames pouring out of the Number Two engine. At least in *Air America* it had been the starboard engine. If that had been the case, she wouldn't have been able to see it from the pilot's seat. Then maybe her copilot Kevin would be rooted to his seat in terror rather than herself.

It was a good thing that it wouldn't be night for another few hours. At night, that fire would look ten times more terrifying...whatever terrifying times ten might actually be.

Pulling the extinguisher, which also cut fuel flow to the engine, hadn't helped. Flames continued to stream out of the cowling. The fact that the tanks still had six thousand pounds per wing of insanely flammable avgas was not encouraging.

There was no refueling planned at Saakow: just a desert combat unload, and a thousand miles back to base. That meant a *lot* of fuel remained in the wing. Explosive fuel in a steel box, sitting in the middle of a fire.

"We're VSF!" Kandace yelled out to Kevin her copilot.

"We're what?"

"Very seriously fucked! *Air America!* Doesn't anyone watch movies around here? Pull Number One."

If the leak was from the feed to the outboard Number One engine...

Kevin pulled the throttle to Number One, cutting the fuel flow, and feathered the prop. She counted to ten—very quickly—and turned to look again.

The fire was growing. That meant that the fuel tanks themselves had been breached by the anti-aircraft rounds.

Kandace triggered the plane's intercom. "So much for

our supply mission. Abandon aircraft. All hands, this is not a drill. Abandon aircraft immediately."

Kevin hesitated; his seat didn't offer a view of the burning port wing.

Kandace just shook her head. "You, too. Get out of here. Make sure my crew is clear, Kevin. Once you're all off, I'll follow."

She couldn't help herself and turned back to look at the wing.

Flames still growing.

Majorly bad.

She wanted another nearby plane to nod at and offer a wry smile the way Richard Dreyfuss had done in *Always*—just before his firefighting plane had disintegrated in mid-air.

So not a good image.

Kevin set the transponder to the emergency frequency. Then he scooted. The last she saw of him was the back of his parachute pack as he hustled out of the cockpit.

She only had two missions now.

One, call in the Mayday. She did. They would scramble search-and-rescue ASAP—from a thousand miles away. Not very helpful, but done.

Two, keep the plane in straight-and-level flight to give her crew the best chance of escape.

A mark on her charts showed the location of the ANISOM military installation in Saakow. That was the best chance for her people.

Taking the risk, she flew over the northwest corner of the town, then hit the internal PA. "Now! Now! Now!"

No way to know if they'd jumped—she didn't dare turn the plane to see. Continuing due west away from the town, she was clear of the houses and farms inside of another minute. Now if her plane exploded, the only person it was going to kill was her.

The Great Waldo Pepper. A Depression-era barnstorming battle between the Red Baron of World War I and an American who never got to be a hero. The inevitable end is never shown, but both pilots know they can never survive landing their critically damaged aircraft as they separately fly into the sunset.

She was going to die in the Somali desert.

Once clear of the town, she started thinking again. Would a landing even be possible? Most of the desert around Saakow had too many scrub trees to land a Hercules.

East of town was her one possible landing zone—a stretch of blood-red desert devoid of any bushes at all. Maybe, if she circled well clear of the town, she might actually be able to land the plane.

That was at least another five to seven minutes of flying time.

One look at the wing and she knew it wasn't going to happen.

Even as Kandace watched, the Number Two engine broke off the wing and tumbled downward into the desert.

Yet the wing still burned furiously.

Time to get out of here.

She set the autopilot—which immediately disengaged. Autopilots weren't made to work when half the plane wasn't functioning.

Out of options, she trimmed the controls for continued flight as well as she could with no functioning engines on the left wing.

Then she slapped her seat's harness release, and raced back through the cockpit.

The fire was lashing in through the open passenger door at the base of the stairs down to the main cargo deck. No sign of burned-up people there, so they must have gotten clear.

Give me a wing and a prayer. It was *Always* again, but that was about as close as she ever got to asking for a little help from the Almighty.

With the stairs blocked and the stench of burning kerosene interfering with her desire to breathe, Kandace jumped over the rail, and landed on a pallet of crates of 5.56 mm ammunition like a beached fish. She groaned and rolled off the pallet and onto the steel cargo deck. Personally, she'd rather have landed on a pallet of bags of rice.

There was light at the far end of the cargo bay.

Some of the crew must have lowered the tail ramp and gotten out that way.

Pushing to her feet she began sprinting for the tail.

Even as she leaned into the sixty-foot dash along the cargo bay, the Hercules began rolling onto its side. In moments, she shifted from sprint to hurdles. Thankfully mostly low ones.

It was like a *Mission: Impossible* scene—she was suddenly running on the walls.

The side of the plane's cargo deck was now downward… and the inside of a C-130 Hercules cargo deck wall was never meant for running.

Hopping over structural ribs.

Praying for sure footing on the round electrical conduits.

Jumping over the emergency water supply like it was a gym class pommel horse. Wow! That was a skill she'd never expected to use again.

As the Hercules nosed down, the incline to the open

ramp fought her, though she was almost there. She could see blue sky.

Wrapping her arms around the rear ramp's massive hydraulic piston, she'd reached the open cargo hatch. Except it was now directly above her.

Looking down, she saw sixty vertical feet of cargo bay stretched out below—a six-story fall.

That's when the wing blew.

A bolt of fire blasted in through the open forward passenger door just below the wing itself.

The first things it hit were the two forward pallets.

Two entire eight-by-nine-foot loads of ammunition stacked four feet high. Rifle and sidearm rounds, grenades, RPG loads, and even some howitzer rounds.

Looking up, she saw the burnt remains of the snapped-off port wing flutter by the open rear cargo hatch.

Kandace didn't know how she did it, but by the time the fireball blasted out the rear of the cargo bay, she was clinging to the outside of the plane just like Tom Cruise in *Mission: Impossible – Rogue Nation.* Except that had been an Airbus A400M Grizzly taking off, not a Lockheed Martin C-130 Hercules busy crashing.

And she definitely needed her head examined.

There were factoids more important than Tom Cruise stunts here—like her imminent death.

Besides, he was old!

Kandace kicked off from the hull as hard as she could.

—and banged her helmet against the underside of the tail.

She tumbled away from the plane.

Blue sky flashing past, then red desert, blue, red—over and over.

2

MEDIC BOB REDFORD COULDN'T STOP FRETTING.

Tonight's mission was only half the reason, but he couldn't help it.

Worse, the two crew chiefs in the back of the MH-60M Black Hawk with him could see it.

And the Delta Operator, an easy stand-in for Megan Fox in *Transformers*, who being true to her role as one of the silent warriors, had said a grand total of one word.

Her squad had been aboard the aircraft carrier. Apparently, she'd heard there was a downed pilot, and had simply stepped aboard his helo as they were scrambling off the deck. The crew chiefs had looked at her askance, but neither one dared to try and throw her off.

Her one word so far? "Carla."

By her accompanying handshake, he'd assumed that was her name, so he offered his own. She'd nodded, lain down on the cargo deck, and gone to sleep with her rifle beside her. A sure sign that she really was what she said she was. Special operations forces could sleep anywhere—especially before a battle.

Which left him alone, wide awake, and fretting.

The CSAR bird wasn't going to go any faster no matter how much he wished it would. A Black Hawk helicopter, even a Night Stalker one, couldn't crack three hundred kilometers an hour. At least it felt as if everything happened faster when he thought in kilometers than loafing along at a mere one-sixty nautical miles an hour. Knots were the worst kind of airspeed because each one seemed to take forever to go by.

"Christ, Bobby!" It took Major Lola Maloney laughing at him from the pilot's seat to make him stop asking if they had any more information every five minutes.

He hated being called Bobby. Though it was better than Robert. Only Mom had ever gotten away with calling him Robert Redford.

"You remind me why I got out of CSAR in the first place. Waiting sucks big-time, doesn't it?" Lola was still laughing.

"Major!" he agreed.

"That's me, Major Pain!"

"No, I didn't mean—" Then he shut up. She *knew* that he'd meant it as a curse rather than impugning her rank. And—palm slapping front of helmet—that's exactly what she was teasing him about.

"She'd rather be in the fight any day," the copilot, Major Tim Maloney, assured him over the headset. Major and Major, a flying couple who led the Night Stalkers 5th Battalion D Company—he couldn't ask for a better transport—even if it was weird that they served on the same bird. Rumor was, they were both so wild that no one else could control them, so command left them together.

That rumor was counteracted by the one that they were the absolute best flying team anywhere in the Night Stalkers since Beale and Henderson retired—whoever they were.

All Bob cared about was that the downed Hercules crew could be bleeding-out somewhere in the Somali wilderness. Lives he could save, if only he could get there fast enough. As soon as he caught himself scrubbing his hands together, he forced himself to stop.

Old habits never died, they just sucked forever!

The other problem was that he still didn't know if this was his final mission. He had yet to sign his re-up papers for another tour. Hanging out on an aircraft carrier waiting for a medic flight had been a full-time occupation during the height of the Iraq and Afghan wars. Now it was a lot of sitting on his ass not being useful.

It had so scratched at his nerves that he'd begged to be dropped out of the back of a C-2 Greyhound small cargo plane just to get to the crash site faster. Greyhounds moved at twice the speed of Black Hawks, but he'd been denied. And there hadn't been any MV-22 Osprey helos available.

"It's fucking Somalia," his commander had informed him. "The zone wasn't supposed to be hot, but apparently it is. You're going to wait for dark and the Night Stalkers will get you in there."

The unspoken part of that statement was that no one else other than the Night Stalkers were *crazy* enough to get him there. And experience had taught him that he wouldn't trust anyone else to make sure he got back out with both his patients' and his own ass intact. So waiting was the right answer, didn't mean that he didn't hate it.

At sunset they'd lifted off the carrier.

Full dark hit as they went feet dry, crossing from the Arabian Sea to over Somali soil. Typical of the Night Stalkers, it seemed as if they were only about five feet over that soil despite the darkness and high speed.

Fifty miles inland, fifteen minutes at full speed.

It felt like hours.

"Hey Bobby?" Tim called out. "Just got word that they've got four of the five crew safe. The Captain kicked them out of a burning plane. Then stayed aboard to down it herself."

"Good news. That's good news."

"Yeah," Tim's voice slowed. "However, word is that the thing went up in a fireball. A ground team of ANISOM guys went out for a look. Thing was blown to hell. But they came under fire and pulled back without a real search. Don't know if she made it."

"We've got to go and look, right?"

"Bring them back, dead or alive," the Delta operator was awake and checking her weapons—as if she hadn't been dead asleep moments before. He'd expected a Delta to be a bristling armory. But she wore just two handguns, a big knife on her thigh, and her rifle. Nothing else. Her vest had a small med kit, a water bottle, two radios, and a lot of extra magazines of ammunition.

"Alive is better," he told her.

"Your job," she nodded. "Mine is making sure *you* come back alive."

"Thanks. I'd appreciate that."

She offered him a sliver of a smile.

As if Delta Carla had woken on some magic cue, the pilot called out. "Two minutes. Then we'll see how fun this is going to be."

3

DUSTY, BURNT, AND BLOODY, SHE'D SWITCHED MOVIES: *AIR America* was now totally *The Flight of the Phoenix.*

Kandace hadn't landed in the fireball of the plane crash—about the only thing that had gone right.

However, the superheated ammo had all lit off the moment that the plane had actually impacted with the desert.

She'd still been descending under her chute, trying to ignore the headache from banging her helmet so hard against the tail's horizontal stabilizer. Kandace forgot about that in short order.

It was the blast of the explosion itself that had driven her clear of the fireball or she just might have landed in the wreck. Of course, it slapped her with a superheated shockwave that had singed her flightsuit almost black. It had also steamed her in it like a tamale in a banana leaf. The LPP, low-profile parachute—designed specifically for pilots and crews of planes without ejection seats—was only moderately steerable. She'd landed at the fireball's whim.

But before that, while she was still aloft, the destruction of all the ammunition had fired a bullet at her.

She'd been shot in the leg—by her own plane. You just couldn't make this stuff up.

Bleeding profusely, she'd landed hard against the broken-off tail empennage she'd banged her head on less than thirty seconds earlier. It had landed less than a hundred feet from the rest of the plane.

The CPR training kicked in first.

Pulling out her survival knife, she slit open the thigh of her flightsuit.

At that moment, a secondary shock wave had caught her still-billowing parachute. It actually lofted her another hundred feet or so into the brush before it snagged on a scrub tree.

She managed to keep her knife, and as a bonus didn't stab herself with it as she was plunged into the nest made by her parachute caught up in the tree's branches.

This time she unharnessed from the chute first.

"You're in the desert, recover everything, Kandace."

And that's how she knew that she and Jimmy Stewart were in the same movie. In *The Flight of the Phoenix* he'd crashed in a Saharan sandstorm hundreds of miles off course. He and the other survivors were going to die in the desert. Their solution? A gargantuan task: rebuilding their twin-engine, twin-boom Fairchild C-82A Packet plane as a simple single-engine monoplane.

Not really an option for her.

Other than the tail section, the largest remaining part of the plane was probably the shot-up Number Two engine, wherever it had fallen.

So, she dropped out of the tree, and managed to drag the

chute down with her. Kandace gauzed her leg with supplies from her survival vest's med kit, then bound it as tightly as she could with a long strip of parachute Kevlar. A tourniquet, alone in the desert, was the same as losing a leg. If she did, she couldn't fly again. Not acceptable. So the binding had better be enough.

The continuing fire and smoke plume, reaching a thousand or more feet into the fading sunset, told her the exact direction of the plane, though it was masked by the scattered trees. Perhaps she'd been blown farther aside than she'd thought.

The plume.

It was etched against the fading afternoon sky.

ANISOM forces would know exactly where to look for her.

Then, from where she lay huddled in the shade of her tree, she saw a battered pickup truck go racing toward the plane. In the back was a circle of men with bandoliers of cartridges and more rifles and RPGs than an entire platoon of Marines.

Al-Shabaab. Maybe she would crawl the other way.

Like Captain Harris in *Phoenix*, she would walk into the desert seeking help she already knew she'd never find. And unlike the Trucker Cobb character, she hoped that she wasn't going to die out here in the dust.

That's when she remembered her radio.

Nothing when she tried it.

She peeled off her helmet. The radio cord was still plugged in.

Following it down she found the emergency radio—half of it anyway.

Kandace rubbed at the line of pain across her chest, a line that passed through the center of the radio. Her chest must have hit the edge of the tail section when she'd first been blown aside from the wreck.

She gave the half-radio and her helmet a quick burial, and a briefer funeral, in the red sand. She'd liked that helmet.

Did it count as a half radio or a no radio? Like in *Wall Street* when Lou tells Bud, "You can't get a little bit pregnant, son." So if it wasn't a half radio, that meant it was...

Kandace shook her head to clear it—and regretted it immediately. Her headache was more like she'd been concussed despite her helmet.

She crawled...away.

Simply...away.

4

"SITE IS EMPTY," THE MAJORS REPORTED. "ZERO HEAT signatures outside the heart of the fire. Not much left of the fire or the plane."

"Maybe she's under something." Bob really hoped so because the other options were beyond anything he could fix. Dead or taken by al-Shabaab.

Carla nodded a maybe. "Drop us half a klick east."

"But—"

"A helo tells any bad guys in the area exactly where we are. I'd rather they didn't meet us at the wreck right away."

Bob supposed that made sense.

"Once you dump us in the dirt," she called to the pilots, "work a ten-klick perimeter. Let us know if anyone is showing undo interest."

"Roger that," Tim called out. "Ground in five, four..."

Bob grabbed his med pack. For a moment he debated between a stretcher and his rifle...but decided he was more likely to need the latter.

The helo didn't actually stop at "One."

A crew chief slid aside the side cargo door. Carla

grabbed the shoulder of his uniform, and they stepped down together. The step that he'd expected to be eighteen inches was five feet.

He did a face-plant into the sand as the helo continued on its way, blasting them with sand and blown grit.

"Those two have a low sense of humor," Carla helped him to his feet.

"Uh, yeah. Sorry." She stayed on her feet despite the unexpected drop. He pulled down the night-vision goggles on his helmet and switched them on.

"In my tracks," she pointed close behind her.

At his nod, she led off, zigzagging until he'd lost all sense of direction. When the plane suddenly loomed before them, it was such a surprise that he almost landed on his face again.

"Not seeing any traps," Carla reported. Which finally explained the crazy back-and-forth course.

He zeroed in on the cockpit. Not much left of it.

"No body," he told her when she joined him. There was also no windshield, but there were parts of the console and the two pilots' seats. "Seat belt is unbuckled. That's a good sign."

Carla nodded.

It took surprisingly little time to inspect the fuselage. The fire had burned hot and hard. There wouldn't have been much identifiable remains left of a pilot. But whatever there might be, they didn't find it. And their safety window here was probably counted in minutes not hours.

"Come on." Carla headed north past the tail section.

"But—" His protest was cut off when she grabbed his sleeve and dragged him under the first trees.

"Sit. Here. Don't move." She was barely five-four, but she

sat his ass down as effortlessly as a six-four MP. Deltas really were a breed apart.

Then she was gone into the night. Even with his night vision on, she seemed to fade from view.

Not daring to move from where she'd planted him, he did his best to make a sector by sector search of the wreckage site. A twist of metal could have been an arm...but wasn't. A curve of a battered tin that might have been a Number 10 can of tomatoes wasn't a helmet. Maybe that—

He yelped when a hand landed on his shoulder from behind.

"Shh!" Carla dragged him to his feet. "I walked the whole perimeter. A lot of tracks in and out, but they're all vehicle tracks. Mostly civilian personnel transport. At least three with tires so bald that they shouldn't still be intact. Lotsa bad guys in pickups. No footprints."

"So she's in there somewhere." He nodded toward the wreckage and tried not to be sick. The chance of Captain Kandace Eversmann surviving that was minimal.

But...he had seen something.

"Hang on." He trotted back toward the tail section.

He'd been right. Bob lifted up the mangled remains of a military-grade radio than had gotten tangled in the sharp edge of the elevator mechanism.

"Do you think al-Shabaab got her?" If they had, the chances of her survival were painfully low.

Carla knelt where he'd found the radio and looked around.

Everything was covered with scorch marks and dust.

"No footprints." Carla rose slowly to her feet inspecting the face of the big tail. It rose almost two stories.

About ten feet up, there was a crease in the leading edge and...

"That's blood splatter," he'd seen the pattern often enough to know it. "Bad wound, but not a spurter." Arterial flow would have smeared over the entire tail section.

"So..." Without explaining, Carla dragged him away from the plane.

"Will you cut that out!"

"Shh!" She stopped a hundred yards from the site. Then she shoved him back—to sit.

"Yeah. Yeah. I get it. Sit, Bob. Stay, Bob. Good boy, Bob."

Carla's smile looked a little feral as it flashed in his night vision. Then she was gone again.

The wait this time was agonizing.

Long enough for him to question why he'd joined the military at all. Because Mom and Dad had both loved the service.

Why had he gone medical? Because Mom's best friend in the Army had died when an IED had taken out her Humvee. Their patrol had no medic because there weren't enough of them. A trained one could have saved her.

Mom had retired and a lot of the life had gone out of her.

Why had he stayed in?

Bob stared back toward the crash site.

Because the first time they'd inserted him into a hot zone, he'd saved two guys' lives. Sent one back to his wife and kids, and the other back to his parents. Maybe not walking tall, but not in body bags either.

He'd done that. A real life-saving hero.

"Top that guys!" He stuck his tongue out at Batman and Superman.

"Careful you don't bite it off," Carla whispered from inches away.

He nearly did in his surprise.

She held up a mangled bit of electronics and a battered helmet. It had an insignia on the side that seemed familiar, but he couldn't place right away.

"What's that?"

"The other half of her radio."

She didn't have to grab his shoulder to get him moving this time.

5

Safety in distance could only motivate her so far. And it had only worked for Katniss Everdeen until fire had chased her back into the game.

Kandace decided it was time to go all-in on *The Hunger Games.* It seemed like a good idea, despite their aircraft being aerodynamically ridiculous, though they cleaned them up a bit by the third installment in the series, *Mockingjay.*

A fresh strip of Kevlar should mask any blood trail.

That gave her an idea.

After cutting off all of the parachute cords and tucking them away in a thigh pouch—on her good leg—she bundled up the Kevlar.

She tossed the parachute off to the side from her earlier track. It unfurled like a red carpet, that happened to be sky blue. Kandace slithered across it.

Much easier than clawing through the gritty sand, she should have thought of this earlier. The water park at the end of *Bill & Ted's Excellent Adventure.* It didn't have any planes, but it did have a great water slide scene. What she wouldn't give for a nice cool water slide at the moment. The desert night might be cooling down, but she couldn't really tell. Maybe she wouldn't feel so hot if she peeled off her flightsuit. Seemed like too much effort.

Instead, she tried to count a flying movie that had been released each year of her life—performing a toss-and-slither once for each film.

Air America and *Die Hard II.* Both in the year she was born. "Damn straight." Slither across the parachute.

Then gather it from behind and toss it ahead. Another parachute length for the second movie.

Memphis Belle. Or had that been the same year. Didn't matter, it was another parachute span from her earlier trail.

She drew a blank for a few years, but *Executive Decision* and *Fly Away Home* meant she had to do two toss-and-slithers for 1996.

Con Air and *Air Force One* gave her another doubleheader.

She kind of forgot to think of any movies until she reached eleven years old: Jodi Foster in *Flightplan.*

What was her own flight plan?

Crawl across the Somali desert all of the way back to Djibouti? A thousand miles of hostile desert and salt pan. One chute-length at a time could take a while.

She wanted to just pull the chute over her like a shroud.

Didn't James Bond do that once to avoid being rescued by a plane at the end of some movie?

Or had he used the Fulton Skyhook where he'd raised a balloon and been swept aloft by a passing B-17 with a massive line catcher on its nose?

Or was that two separate movies?

Why couldn't she remember?

And maybe...

She reached for her water bottle. But it wasn't in her thigh pocket.

Kandace had been parsing out the water by the scant mouthful, but no matter where she looked it was gone.

It had been…

She reached for the thigh pocket again and had to bite back a scream when she grabbed her wound.

On the other side, she found the correct pocket, and pulled out…paracord.

She'd taken a drink while cutting the cords off her parachute. The bundled cord had gone into the empty pocket.

Then she'd slip-slid away, with the comforting pressure of a half bottle still in its place.

Except it was back there.

In the sand.

She couldn't even be sure of the direction.

Kandace managed one final toss-and-crossing. But lost in the desert without any water, she knew that even James Bond wasn't going to get her out of this one.

It took everything she had left to dig a hole in the sand, line it with the chute, and lay in it. It was tricky, but she managed to bury herself.

With only her face showing, she felt the world closing around her.

It was quiet. Peaceful.

Like the end of *Top Gun.* Hopefully without the ending credit in memory of the stunt pilot who'd died during the filming of the flat spin.

6

"We're pushing on time here," Tim called down from their helo. "We've got a company-sized force moving in your direction, and ANISOM confirms it isn't them."

"Roger that," was all Carla answered.

The trail had been easy to follow, though a steady onshore wind was erasing the tracks fast enough to be a real challenge soon.

Carla double-timed her way forward.

Bob did what he could to keep pace with her.

They were getting closer. He'd seen the heat along her track...the heat of blood.

By the amount he'd seen smeared on the plane's tail, and then again where her trail had magically appeared on the ground, he knew she'd be tapped out soon. Any rational person would have stopped long ago.

There was a tenacity there that he really appreciated. It reminded him of why he did this. Of why he'd stayed in, at least so far.

She'd become a talisman for him.

If he could save her, then he'd know that he was doing exactly what he was supposed to be doing.

If not? Well, maybe there really was a reason he hadn't signed his re-up papers yet. Maybe he'd see what the civilian side was like. Be like Batman and drop out of the superhero business—with a girl he didn't have.

"Shit!"

This time he did run into Carla's back and knocked them both to the sand.

She didn't even complain.

"What's the problem?" he asked when he saw her scouting around.

"The trail just ended."

"Just...ended?"

"Listen to my words. Ended. As in doesn't continue," Carla sounded pissed. An angry Delta operator was not a good sign.

Bob began scouting as well. Behind a low thorn bush he found two things: a water bottle, and the tip of a bloody Kevlar strip sticking up out of the sand.

He inspected the latter carefully. "Point wound. Not a slice. The stain pattern says that the wound was covered in gauze. That's one tough pilot."

"One tough pilot who is out at the edge enough that she forgot her water."

"But figured out how to disappear," he reminded her.

There was no heat signature under the bush or up any of the few nearby scrub trees. Their night-vision goggles were sensitive enough that they should be able to trace even a footprint for several hours after it was made.

Nothing.

This time it was Major Lola, the mission commander,

who called them. “They’ll be on the site in five. Hot on your trail in six. We’re running out of options, folks.”

“Acknowledge,” was all Carla said.

Kandace was close. Somewhere, somehow, Captain Kandace Eversmann was seriously close.

The breeze was strong enough that it blew a hot ochre breath of dust that was unavoidable.

He raised his goggles and wiped his eyes clear of sand.

It was blackest night. Not like night on a well-lit military base or even just dark. It was pitch black. The nearest lights would be from the town miles away. A town too small and primitive to have streetlights.

With the state Somalia was in, power might even be a rarity.

Nothing to see.

No sign of any track.

The only light was a faint green trace that the goggles cast around Carla’s eyes.

“We found her helmet.”

“Buried,” Carla agreed.

“No NVGs, how is she navigating?”

“Flashlight.”

“No,” Bob looked around again. “She knows someone is after her. She’s fully night adapted and navigating by shadow and starlight.”

“That still doesn’t explain how she’s hid her track.”

Bob wasn’t sure, but maybe it did in some strange way.

“If someone is tracking you, the best thing you can do is look like something else. And go in an unexpected direction. Right?”

Carla went quiet.

Bob dropped his NVGs back into place. “Like *Butch Cassidy and the Sundance Kid.* Both jumping onto the same horse wasn't enough to fool the trackers. But becoming payroll guards in Bolivia, and going straight, had been the perfect disguise, until it wasn't."

"Never saw it. Don't do movies much."

"She went sideways here," Bob pointed at the water bottle, which had been behind a bush from the direction the track had been taking.

And now that he'd said it, he could see it. "The sand is too smooth. Like a road roller went over it."

He didn't wait for Carla. Now that he'd seen it, he broke into a run.

It went straight for fifty meters, but then the path started to wander. Finally, he had to slow down, just to negotiate the odd jinks and turns.

He prayed that it wasn't what he thought it was—the pilot's brain shutting down through lack of blood.

When he hit a line of sand ripples, he spun around. Every direction was rippled except the one he'd come from. *End of trail.*

"She's here." But no matter which way he looked...she wasn't here. Had she found some new way to evaporate into thin air?

"Now would be good," Lola called down from the helo. He could hear it passing nearby. There was an absolute calm in her voice, so different from her earlier tone that it told him just how tight time was becoming.

"I know she's here. I just need a moment," he told Carla.

She nodded once. Then she was moving back the way they'd come.

Not knowing what else to do, Bob sat in the last clear flat spot.

Behind him was the path he'd followed here.

Just like at the plane, he scanned a slow circle but didn't see anything.

Yet he knew she was here.

Here but disguised...even from the heat sensitive eyes of night vision.

Like Arnold Schwarzenegger in *Predator.* He'd hidden himself from the Predator's infrared vision with mud.

How to do that in the desert?

He smacked his forehead.

She wasn't here.

She was *under* here—buried in the sand.

The only thing exposed would be her face or a breathing vent if she'd gone really extreme. He lay down and looked under every bush and clump of grass.

At a loud burst from a machine gun and the hard *Crump!* of an RPG explosion, he spun around to face the way they'd come. That would be Carla running interference.

Because he was still on his belly, he saw it.

A warm mound of sand, underneath a bush, one smooth patch back in the direction they'd come from.

His missing Captain Kandace had doubled back to hide her trail.

He took a second for a short radio message. "Got her." The firefight didn't abate and he didn't have time to care.

Unearthed, her breathing was slow and shallow, but the pulse was there.

No point in taking her blood pressure, he knew there wouldn't be enough blood in her to give the numbers any meaning. He fished out her dog tags to check her blood type. Good. He had her covered.

As he tapped a unit of blood from his pack into one arm and a unit of saline into the other—finding the veins was a bitch—there was a vast barrage from above.

He looked up and saw a strange sight.

The Black Hawk helicopter might be nearly invisible, even in the NVGs. But the twin snakes of fire that the crew chiefs' miniguns were unleashing like Wonder Woman's Lasso of Truth stood out in brilliant green.

He laughed.

Of course. That was the emblem on the side of the pilot's helmet: the stacked golden Ws of Wonder Woman.

He jabbed a local into her leg unsure of what else she'd dosed herself with. He checked her med kit, but it still had the standard stock of two fentanyl suckers. So maybe she was on nothing.

Damn but that was strong.

Once he unwrapped her leg, he knew he was in the presence of greatness. She'd ministered to herself, moved hundreds of meters, fooled a Delta operator, and hidden with the skill of Arnold. Doing it all with a nightmare wound in her leg. Whatever metal had gone into her had been tumbling, and drilled a nasty hole.

For now, he pulled out a sponge injector, shot a half dozen into the open wound, and re-bound it as the sponges expanded to congeal blood and release antiseptics.

Captain Kandace Eversmann groaned herself awake as the sharp hiss of launching rockets sounded from the Black Hawk somewhere overhead. The brightness of their impacts lit the sparse terrain. It was a bad night to be taking on the Night Stalkers in Somalia.

"Hey, Sleeping Beauty." And she was. There hadn't been time to notice that before.

"She'sh...blonde," Kandace mumbled. "I'm brun-ette."

"Right now your hair is the red color of sand. Eversmann, like *Black Hawk Down* Eversmann?" He wanted to keep her talking. Make sure her brain was still functioning.

"Second cousin, I shink. Never met him. Kinda weird seeing him in the film. Part of the reashon I joint. Joined." Her speech was getting better—a little. Still slurred, but a good sign.

"Burying yourself was *Predator* slick." Now he checked her vitals. Blood pressure low but rising. Pupils responsive to the flashes of the firefight going on overhead.

"Peeta in—"

"*The Hunger Games.* Same trick. It worked. Almost too well. Made you damn hard to find."

She squinted up at him.

"What did you do to hide your trail? You totally confused a Delta Operator, just so you know."

That earned him a lopsided smile that added a bright humor to her face. She began singing, soft and hoarse at first, it took him a moment to pick out the tune.

"*Waterloo?* Like ABBA? No, not *Mama Mia.*"

She shook her head and kept singing. Damn but he could get to like that smile. He changed out the empty blood bag for a second unit.

"Wait a sec. *Bill & Ted's Excellent Adventure.* Uh, the water slide scene at the end. Yeah, okay. Your track was wide and flat like a water slide, but you're in the middle of the desert. I still don't get it."

"Sliding. On parachute," her voice caught hard, and he fed her just a sip of water. Muscle control would be slow to return and he didn't want her choking on it. On her third try, she managed to pluck at the fabric that spread beneath her.

"Damn, you really are Wonder Woman."

"Name," she croaked out and he fed her another sip of water.

"Your name is Captain Kandace Eversmann. Not all that far from Katniss Everdeen. No wonder you remembered Peeta's hiding trick before Schwarzenegger's."

She grimaced at his tease of telling her *her* own name as she took another swallow.

"Sergeant Bob Redford."

Kandace spat her water into his face, then coughed and choked on it.

"Didn't think it was that bad."

"Robert...Redshferd."

He sighed. "No relation that I know of. I'm named for my Uncle Bob. Died in the service the week before I was born."

7

KANDACE HAD MANAGED NOT TO CRY OUT AS THEY SHIFTED her onto the stretcher and lifted her into the hovering helo.

Bob Redford. She still couldn't get over that, her parents were going to laugh their asses off—Mom had a major crush on his non-namesake.

Their tastes had overlapped for superhero movies, but where she'd gone in for flying, he'd always followed science fiction—a blank to her beyond *Star Trek* because, hey, Zachary Quinto was seriously cute.

Bob Redford might not look anything like his namesake, but there was a slight resemblance to Mr. Spock that she could seriously like.

When she woke on the aircraft carrier after the surgeons had re-jiggered her leg, he was leaning on the empty infirmary bed next to hers.

"Just like *The Horse Whisperer,* they say you're too good a pilot to put down. Instead, you've got some new nano-tubing in your leg, so you're now *The Bionic Woman.* You're going to be able to fly again."

It was the first thing she needed to hear and he was kind

enough to know that. She'd managed not to think about that over the hours she'd been crawling across the desert. But at the news, she couldn't help the tears that slipped down her cheeks.

"That's good news," she managed to choke out as he dabbed at her cheeks with a tissue. "Really good news."

"What? No snappy movie reference?" His smile said he couldn't think of one either.

She could only shake her head.

"I don't like that sad look at all. Doesn't fit you for a second, Kandace."

"I like you," it just slipped out before she could stop it.

"Mutual, lady. Wonder Woman who is a pilot and a movie fiend? Yeah, a lot to like."

Kandace had always found that it was far too easy to imagine Wonder Woman going into a future—in which her true love Steve Trevor is dead and gone. Well, true love might happen someday, but there was a major obstacle with the man who'd used movies to save her life.

Once she was returned to flight status, she'd be back to her Air Force posting. And when Bob had returned to the Army's Night Stalkers, they'd probably never see each other again.

Unsure what else to do, she pointed at herself then him. "Air Force. Army."

He made the same gesture, himself then her. "Air Force. Air Force. Night Stalkers were just giving me a ride. Plus a little help from Delta."

"You're Air Force?"

Bob nodded. And damn but he liked that lop-sided smile on her. Especially now that he knew it natural and not blood-loss induced.

"How would you feel about being a flying medic on my

new Hercules, when I get one? I fly mostly humanitarian missions."

Bob could feel his own smile.

That's when he realized that he'd been *looking* for a reason to re-up. Like Kirk in the *Star Trek* reboot. Joining because it was what he was meant to do.

And flying with Kandace?

Chris Pine had played both Steve Trevor to Wonder Woman as well as Captain Kirk who always got the girl—except Chris Pine never did.

Finding a way to fly through life with Kandace? Seriously cool plot twist!

Be sure to keep reading to see an excerpt from the exciting Night Stalkers White House series.

DANIEL'S CHRISTMAS (EXCERPT)

IF YOU ENJOYED THIS STORY, YOU'LL LOVE THIS SERIES!

DANIEL'S CHRISTMAS (EXCERPT)

DANIEL DRAKE DARLINGTON III PUSHED BACK FURTHER INTO the armchair and hung on for dear life. Without warning the seat did its best to eject him forcibly onto the floor. Only the heavy seatbelt, that was threatening to cut him in half he'd pulled it so tight, kept him in place.

"You never were the best flier."

Daniel glared at President Peter Matthews as Marine One jolted sharply left. They occupied the two facing armchairs in the narrow cargo bay of the VH-1N White Hawk helicopter. The small, three-person couch along the side was empty. The two Marine Corps crew chiefs and the two pilots sat in their seats at the front of the craft.

"I'm fine," Daniel managed through gritted teeth. "I just don't like helicopters."

President Peter Matthews sat back casually. Apparently all the turbulence that the early winter storm could hand out had not interfered with his boss' enjoyment of Daniel's discomfiture.

"And why would that be?"

The President knew damn well why his Chief of Staff

hated these god-forsaken machines. Even if Marine One was probably the single safest and best maintained helicopter on the planet, he hated it from the depths of his soul along with all of its brethren of the rotorcraft category.

"My very first flight. I suffered—" a jaw rattling shake, "a bad concussion. Then we crashed."

"Yes," the President stared contemplatively at the ceiling less than foot over their heads.

Daniel kept his head ducked down so that he didn't bang it there as they flew through the next pocket of winter turbulence.

"That was one of Emily's finer flights."

And it had been. If the helicopter had been flown by anyone of lesser skill than Major Emily Beale of the Special Operations Aviation Regiment, Daniel knew he'd have been dead rather than merely bruised and battered. Thankfully the Army trained the pilots of the 160th SOAR exceptionally well, even better than the four Marines flying the President's personal craft. And Major Beale was the best among them, except for perhaps her husband.

The tape of that flight and the much more fateful flight a bare two weeks later had become mandatory training in the Army's Special Operations Forces helicopter regiment. To this day he knew his life would have ended if he'd been aboard for that second fiery crash. The crash that had taken the First Lady's life a year ago.

But that didn't make him like this machine one whit better.

"There's home." President Matthews nodded out the window just like any tourist. Any tourist who was allowed to fly over the intensely restricted airspace surrounding the White House.

Daniel managed to look toward the window as the

helicopter banked sharply to the left. Please, just let them land safely and get out of this storm. The White House did look terribly cheery. November 30th, she wasn't sporting her Christmas décor yet, but she was a majestic building, brilliantly lit, perched in the middle of the most heavily guarded park on the planet. Another jolt and he squeezed his eyes shut.

He did manage to force his eyes open as they settled flawlessly onto the lawn with barely the slightest rocking on the shock absorbers.

In moments the door slid open and a pair of Marines stood at sharp attention in their dress uniforms as if the last day of November were a sunny summer day, and not blowing freezing rain at eleven o'clock at night.

Daniel stumbled out and managed to resist the urge to kneel and kiss the ground. For one thing, it would stain the knees of his suit. For another, the President would laugh at him. Okay, he'd laugh even more than he already was.

Both feet on the ground, Daniel found himself. Managed to pull on his Chief-of-Staff cloak so to speak. He grabbed his briefcase and kept his place beside the President as they headed toward the South Entrance. They each carried umbrellas of only marginal usefulness that the Marines had thoughtfully provided. Now that they were on the ground, Daniel didn't mind the cold rain in his face. It meant he was alive.

"I'd suggest turning in right away, sir. We have an early start tomorrow."

The President clapped him on the shoulder, "Yes, Mom."

"Your mother is over in Georgetown."

"Well, I'm not going to call you 'dear' so don't get your hopes up there."

Daniel had come to really like the President. Even at the

end of a brutally long day, including a flight to Kansas City, then Chicago, and back, he remained upbeat with that indefatigable energy of his. He was easy to like. There'd now be no oil workers' strike in Kansas City and his Chicago dinner speech had benefited the new governor immensely.

"You go to bed too, Daniel."

"Just going to drop off this paperwork," he held up his briefcase.

The President headed for the Grand Staircase and Daniel turned down the white marble hall and headed over to the West Wing.

Somewhere behind them in the dark, the helicopter roared back to life and lifted into the night.

THE PHONE HAMMERED HIM AWAKE. DANIEL CAME TO IN HIS office chair with the phone already to his ear.

Someone was speaking rapidly. He caught perhaps one word in three. "CIA. Immediate briefing. North Korea."

He must have made some intelligible reply as moments later he was listening to a dial tone.

Daniel rubbed at his eyes, but the vista didn't change. Large cherry wood desk. Mounds of work in neatly stacked folders that he'd sat down to tackle after the long flight. His briefcase still unopened on the floor beside him. Definitely the Chief of Staff's office. His office. Nightmare or reality? Both. Definitely.

Phone. He'd been on the phone.

The words came back and, now fully awake, Daniel started swearing even as he grabbed the handset and began dialing.

Maybe he could blame all this on Emily Beale. In the

three short weeks she'd been at the White House, Daniel had risen from being the First Lady's secretary to the White House Chief of Staff and it was partly Emily's fault. As if his life had been battered by a tornado. Still felt that way a year later.

Okay, call it mostly her fault.

As he listened to the phone ringing in his ear, it felt better to have someone to blame. He rubbed at his eyes. A year later and he still didn't know whether to curse Major Beale or thank her.

Maybe he could make it all her fault.

"Yagumph."

"Good morning, Mr. President."

"Is it morning?" The deep voice would have been incomprehensibly groggy without the familiarity of long practice.

Daniel checked his watch, barely morning. "Yes, sir!" he offered his most chipper voice.

"Crap! What? All of 12:03?"

"12:10, sir." They'd been on the ground just over an hour.

"Double crap!" The President was slowly gaining in clarity, maybe one in ten linguists would be able to understand him now.

"Seven more minutes of sleep than you guessed, sir."

"Daniel?"

"Yes, Mr. President?"

"Next time Major Beale comes to town, I'm sending you up on one of her training rides."

"Sounds like fun, sir." If he had a death wish. "Crashing in the Lincoln Memorial Reflecting Pool is definitely an experience I can't wait to relive." The Major was also the childhood friend of the President, so he had to walk with a little care, but not much. The two of them were that close.

"Time to get up, sir, the CIA is coming calling. They'll be here in twenty minutes."

"I'll be there in ten." A low groan sounded over the phone. "Make that fifteen." The handset rattled loudly as he missed the cradle. Daniel got the phone clear of his ear before the President's handset dropped on the floor.

Keep reading at fine retailers everywhere!
Daniel's Christmas

ABOUT THE AUTHOR

USA Today and Amazon #1 Bestseller M. L. "Matt" Buchman started writing on a flight south from Japan to ride his bicycle across the Australian Outback. Just part of a solo around-the-world trip that ultimately launched his writing career.

From the very beginning, his powerful female heroines insisted on putting character first, *then* a great adventure. He's since written over 60 action-adventure thrillers and military romantic suspense novels. And just for the fun of it: 100 short stories, and a fast-growing pile of read-by-author audiobooks.

Booklist says: "3X Top 10 of the Year." PW says: "Tom Clancy fans open to a strong female lead will clamor for more." His fans say: "I want more now...of everything." That his characters are even more insistent than his fans is a hoot.

As a 30-year project manager with a geophysics degree who has designed and built houses, flown and jumped out of planes, and solo-sailed a 50' ketch, he is awed by what is possible. More at: www.mlbuchman.com.

Other works by M. L. Buchman: *(* - also in audio)*

Action-Adventure Thrillers

Dead Chef
One Chef!
Two Chef!

Miranda Chase
*Drone**
*Thunderbolt**
*Condor**
*Ghostrider**

Romantic Suspense

Delta Force
*Target Engaged**
*Heart Strike**
*Wild Justice**
*Midnight Trust**

Firehawks
MAIN FLIGHT
Pure Heat
Full Blaze
*Hot Point**
*Flash of Fire**
Wild Fire
SMOKEJUMPERS
*Wildfire at Dawn**
*Wildfire at Larch Creek**
*Wildfire on the Skagit**

The Night Stalkers
MAIN FLIGHT
The Night Is Mine
I Own the Dawn
Wait Until Dark
Take Over at Midnight
Light Up the Night
Bring On the Dusk
By Break of Day
AND THE NAVY
Christmas at Steel Beach
Christmas at Peleliu Cove
WHITE HOUSE HOLIDAY
*Daniel's Christmas**
*Frank's Independence Day**
*Peter's Christmas**
*Zachary's Christmas**
*Roy's Independence Day**
*Damien's Christmas**
5E
Target of the Heart
Target Lock on Love
Target of Mine
Target of One's Own

Shadow Force: Psi
*At the Slightest Sound**
*At the Quietest Word**
*At the Merest Glance**
*At the Clearest Sensation**

White House Protection Force
*Off the Leash**
*On Your Mark**
*In the Weeds**

Contemporary Romance

Eagle Cove
Return to Eagle Cove
Recipe for Eagle Cove
Longing for Eagle Cove
Keepsake for Eagle Cove

Henderson's Ranch
*Nathan's Big Sky**
*Big Sky, Loyal Heart**
*Big Sky Dog Whisperer**

Love Abroad
Heart of the Cotswolds: England
Path of Love: Cinque Terre, Italy

Other works by M. L. Buchman:

Contemporary Romance (cont)

Where Dreams

Where Dreams are Born
Where Dreams Reside
*Where Dreams Are of Christmas**
Where Dreams Unfold
Where Dreams Are Written

Science Fiction / Fantasy

Deities Anonymous

Cookbook from Hell: Reheated
Saviors 101

Single Titles

The Nara Reaction
Monk's Maze
the Me and Elsie Chronicles

Non-Fiction

Strategies for Success

Managing Your Inner Artist/Writer
*Estate Planning for Authors**
Character Voice
*Narrate and Record Your Own Audiobook**

Short Story Series by M. L. Buchman:

Romantic Suspense

Delta Force

Th Delta Force Shooters
The Delta Force Warriors

Firehawks

The Firehawks Lookouts
The Firehawks Hotshots
The Firebirds

The Night Stalkers

The Night Stalkers
The Night Stalkers 5E
The Night Stalkers CSAR
The Night Stalkers Wedding Stories

US Coast Guard

White House Protection Force

Contemporary Romance

Eagle Cove

Henderson's Ranch*

Where Dreams

Action-Adventure Thrillers

Dead Chef

Miranda Chase Origin

Science Fiction / Fantasy

Deities Anonymous

Other

The Future Night Stalkers
Single Titles

SIGN UP FOR M. L. BUCHMAN'S NEWSLETTER TODAY

and receive:
Release News
Free Short Stories
a Free Book

Get your free book today. Do it now.
free-book.mlbuchman.com

www.ingramcontent.com/pod-product-compliance
Lightning Source LLC
LaVergne TN
LVHW050944080826
845145LV00004B/1400

* 9 7 8 1 9 4 9 8 2 5 9 3 0 *